For Lori, who got this whole thing started.
—A. Z.

STERLING CHILDREN'S BOOKS
New York

An Imprint of Sterling Publishing Co., Inc.
1166 Avenue of the Americas
New York, NY 10036

ISBN 978-1-4549-2114-1

Distributed in Canada by Sterling Publishing Co., Inc.
c/o Canadian Manda Group, 664 Annette Street
Toronto, Ontario, Canada M6S 2C8
Distributed in the United Kingdom by GMC Distribution Services
Castle Place, 166 High Street, Lewes, East Sussex, England BN7 1XU
Distributed in Australia by NewSouth Books
45 Beach Street, Coogee, NSW 2034, Australia

For information about custom editions, special sales, and premium and corporate purchases,
please contact Sterling Special Sales at 800-805-5489 or specialsales@sterlingpublishing.com.

Manufactured in China
Lot #:
2 4 6 8 10 9 7 5 3 1
01/17

www.sterlingpublishing.com

Design by Irene Vandervoort

Dance Is for Everyone

Words and Pictures by ANDREA ZUILL

STERLING CHILDREN'S BOOKS
New York

Mrs. Iraina and her ballerinas were surprised.

There was a new student in their dance class.

They decided it was okay for her to join.
(Besides, who would be brave enough to tell
a 450-pound alligator she couldn't?)

She didn't understand what was being said,
but she was great at following along.

They were pleased that she didn't try to eat anyone, not even a nibble.

Still, precautions were taken just in case the new student got hungry.

After a while, they got used to having an alligator in their class.

They started calling her Tanya because she bore a resemblance to the great prima ballerina Madame Tanya Prefontaine.

Tanya liked that a lot.

Much like Madame Prefontaine, Tanya was very
strong. A bit too strong.

And she didn't seem to know what
was going on with her tail.

The studio got a lot smaller when there was an
alligator dancing in it.

It was a problem!

But what could they do?

They didn't want to hurt her feelings. That might
make her grumpy or bitey.

Besides, they didn't speak alligator.

Mrs. Iraina and the students came up
with an idea.

They would create a dance for someone
who was very large, very enthusiastic . . . and had
a big, swishy tail.

The next week they started learning the new dance. It was
called "The Legend of the Swamp Queen."

Tanya was overjoyed to have the lead role (the Swamp Queen). Mrs. Iraina and the other students were happy to see her having so much fun.

Also, they loved not getting hit by her tail.

It was going so well that they agreed that "The Legend of the Swamp Queen" would be the perfect piece for their upcoming recital.

Giggle!

On the big night, everyone giggled
with nervous excitement.

Then the dance started.

So when Tanya didn't show up for the next class,
they wondered why.

Weeks went by, and Tanya was still missing.
Then, one day, they received an invitation
to a very special performance.

The audience loved it!